The Wonderful World of Disney

Walt Disney

THE FOX
AND
THE HOUND

Twin Books

DERRYDALE BOOKS
New York

Pursued by hunters, a mother fox left her cub in the safety of a nearby farm.

Mrs. Tweed was hanging out her laundry when a gust of wind blew a cloth from the line over to where the cub lay. She went to fetch the cloth and was startled to find the little fox.

"Oh! A baby fox!" she cried, picking up the frightened animal. "You must have been abandoned." The kind lady hugged the cub and carried him into the house. She prepared some milk for him and said, "I'll take good care of you! Your name will be Tod."

Near Mrs. Tweed's farm lived a hunter called Amos Slade. The same day that Mrs. Tweed found Tod, Amos brought home a puppy as a surprise for his old hound, Chief. "His name is Copper," announced Amos. "You can teach him how to hunt."

Chief was a brave hunting hound. He was proud of the many rabbits, raccoons and foxes he had helped his master catch. "What am I going to do with a silly little puppy?" he grumbled.

When the puppy licked the big dog on the nose, Chief softened. "Well, just do what I say," Chief added, "and we'll get along."

5

Copper won the big hound's heart. Whenever Chief lay down for a nap, Copper would snuggle up against Chief and sleep, too. Chief even shared his food with the puppy. The old hound enjoyed his little friend's company.

At the farm, Mrs. Tweed was enjoying the company of her little friend, too. Every day she fed Tod a bottle of milk, holding him like a baby. In the evenings when she sat knitting, she would smile at Tod, who gently played with her yarn.

As time went by, Tod grew a little bigger and stronger. He was happy. But he often looked out the window, longing to go outside and explore.

Mrs. Tweed sensed the little fox's desire and one day let Tod out of the house. Tod ventured away from the farm and into the woods. He was delighted by all the new sights and sounds. He smelled the flowers and chased a butterfly.

Copper had also grown bigger, and
longed to play in the woods, too.
Although Copper loved Chief, the old
hound just couldn't keep up with the
frisky puppy.

So Copper decided to play in the woods.
He busily sniffed the exciting new scents.

Copper began to trail one particular scent, which soon led
him through a large hollow log. At the other end of the log, he
suddenly ran into Tod, who had been sniffing along the top of
the same log. "He's a funny-looking dog," thought Copper. "But
maybe he'll play with me.

Every day thereafter the fox and the
hound romped in the woods together,
laughing and chasing each other.

11

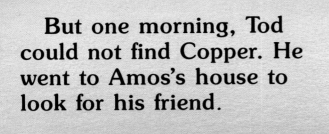

But one morning, Tod could not find Copper. He went to Amos's house to look for his friend.

Tod was surprised to find Copper tied to a doghouse made from a barrel. Mrs. Tweed never tied *him* up. Tod tried to pull his friend away to play when he spotted old Chief, lying asleep in another barrel.

"He looks like a nice old fellow," Tod said to Copper.

Tod approached Chief to play. But the old hound, recognizing the scent of his enemy the fox, woke up growling.

Chief suddenly lunged at Tod and chased the frightened fox around the yard. Hens clucked and fluttered in all directions.

Thinking that someone was stealing his chickens, Amos ran over and fired a shot. Tod leaped over the fence and raced home to safety.

For a long time, Tod and Copper did not see one another. Meanwhile, Amos was determined to make Copper into a hunting hound. Even in the snow, Amos and Chief would bring Copper along on hunts up in the mountains.

By the end of the winter, Copper had
grown almost to Chief's size. Copper felt
the urge to hunt and had learned to
recognize many kinds of scents. Chief and
Amos were pleased with Copper's progress.

When Copper was smaller, Chief used to sit in the front of the car next to Amos. But soon Copper had the front-seat honor. Chief had to ride in the back.

Every day the trio would drive off to hunt, Amos crooning and Copper howling happily.

By now Tod was a full-grown, handsome fox. But he was a lonely fox, who missed his friend Copper. One day he decided to visit Copper, in spite of his fear of Chief and Amos. Copper recognized his old friend, but was not happy to see him.

"I'm sorry, Tod. I can't be your friend anymore," said Copper firmly. "I was born to hunt your kind."

Tod was confused and disappointed.

19

Just then Chief awoke, smelling the fox. The old hound started to bark, pulling at his chain. Tod jumped back, remembering all too well how Chief had chased him once before.

Chief's barking signaled Amos, who shot at Tod. The fox panicked and zigzagged through the field, running as fast as he could.

Tod climbed a little hill and skidded down a slope. Quickly he slipped underneath a pile of lumber next to some railroad tracks. He was shaking with fear when Copper came up to him. "Amos and Chief are after you," he warned. "Go up the tracks. I led them the other way."

"Good luck!" Copper said, and he left.
Tod was glad that Copper was his friend,
after all. He followed Copper's advice,
running up the railroad tracks to the bridge.

But Chief had not been fooled by Copper's diversion. The old hound was waiting at the bridge when Tod arrived. Chief started to bark triumphantly.

All of a sudden a thundering noise shook the bridge. A train was heading toward them at top speed. Tod instinctively flattened himself between the rails. The train passed over without harming him. Chief had jumped desperately to the side, but fell off the bridge to the ravine below.

Tod slowly made his way to Mrs.
Tweed's farm, all the time hoping that
Chief would be all right.

When Tod arrived back at home, he
slipped into his foster mother's arms for
comfort. He was very weary and lay down in
his comfortable bed. "At least Copper is still
my friend," Tod thought as he fell asleep.

But Copper was filled with anger toward Tod. He blamed the fox for Chief's injury and vowed revenge.

Amos had stomped over to Mrs. Tweed, threatening to avenge his hurt hound. In order to protect Tod from her angry neighbor, Mrs. Tweed brought him to a wildlife sanctuary, which permitted no hunters.

Mrs. Tweed took off Tod's collar, saying, "I hope you make many friends here. You'll be very happy."

After Mrs. Tweed left, Tod was very confused. He could not understand why she had taken him away from his home. "What will I do now?" he thought sadly. "I'm all alone." He walked slowly into the strange forest.

After wandering aimlessly, Tod lay down near a clump of bushes and drifted off to sleep.

Tod thought he was dreaming when he was awakened by a lovely girl fox. She smiled and said, "I'm Vixey. What's your name?" Tod thought, "How beautiful she is!"

"My. . . my name is Tod," he said shyly. They were in love.

Above on a branch, Big Mama the owl, Dinky the sparrow and Boomer the woodpecker watched them. "What a handsome couple," sighed Big Mama.

Back at Amos's house, Chief was
resting with his hurt leg in a bandage.

Mrs. Tweed had informed Amos that Tod was now in a wildlife sanctuary and would not bother him anymore.

Amos fetched his gun, some pliers, and Copper. They headed for the sanctuary. "That wicked fox won't get away!" Amos snapped. "Sanctuary or no sanctuary!"

Amos used pliers to cut the barbed wire that surrounded the sanctuary, and he and Copper slipped through. Copper quickly sniffed out Tod's scent and found the foxes, sitting on a grassy knoll.

Copper bounded after them and barked threateningly. Vixey sprang back in fear.

Tod's wild instincts were aroused. He was determined to protect Vixey.

Former friends, the fox and the hound now faced each other as enemies, growling fiercely.

Amos came running up and fired some shots. The startled foxes bolted. "Let's go to my burrow!" Vixey shouted as they ran. She led them down a hill and into the opening of her home. Tod and Vixey huddled together. Tod was prepared to attack, should Amos and Copper find them.

The hunter and the hound had spotted the foxes leaping into the burrow.

"Now we have them!" said Amos confidently.

Suddenly a great roar made Amos shake in his boots with terror.

A huge grizzly bear, who had been foraging nearby, was angry at the hunter's intrusion. The bear stood on his hind legs, towering over Amos.

Amos tried to shoot the bear but
missed. The blast angered the bear even
more. The panic-stricken hunter began to
step backward and tripped over a rock.
He fell to the ground, screaming.

Tod heard the screams and ventured out of the burrow. When he saw Copper and Amos in danger, he thought of attacking the bear.

Copper had tried to defend Amos by lunging at the bear. But the grizzly struck him to the ground.

"I've got to rescue Copper," thought Tod. "I can't abandon him. He was my friend."

Tod swiftly pounced and bit the bear on the head. The raving mad grizzly began chasing Tod. The fox led the bear towards the river away from Amos and Copper.

At the river, Tod darted onto an old tree trunk that hung over the rapids. The bear followed him over the water, cornering his prey.

But the trunk, rotted by age, gave way with a loud crack. Both the bear and the fox crashed into the torrent below. The bear hit a rock and fell silent.

Tod swirled around in the water. Using
the last of his strength, he swam ashore.
He was exhausted.

When Tod looked up, Amos loomed over him with his raised shotgun. Tod stared in disbelief. He had saved the hunter's life! Would Amos shoot him after all? The fox was too weary to move. He lay still, resigned to his fate.

Just then Copper jumped in front of Tod. The hound was grateful that Tod had so bravely saved their lives.

"If Amos shoots you, he'll have to shoot me too," Copper said to Tod.

Amos was confused and thought for a minute. Then he lowered his gun. "Copper, you're right. Your friend should go free," said Amos. "Thanks for saving us, little fox."

With that remark, Amos turned to go.
"Good-bye, Tod, and thank you!" called
Copper, looking back at the fox.
"Good-bye, Copper," said Tod, glad that
they were friends again.

Tod went back to Vixey.

The two foxes were very happy together. They often sat on the cliff overlooking the valley and thought about their friends below.

"Do you know what are the two best things in the world?" Tod once asked Vixey. "Love and friendship," he answered. She agreed.

This 1988 edition published by Derrydale Books, distributed by Crown Publishers, Inc., 225 Park Avenue South New York, New York 10003

Directed by HELENA Productions Ltd. Image adaptation by Van Gool-Lefevre-Loiseaux

Produced by Twin Books 15 Sherwood Place Greenwich, CT 06830

Printed and bound in Hong Kong

ISBN 0-517-67007-0

The Wonderful World of Disney